Dalmatian Press, LLC, 2002. All rights reserved. Printed in the U.S.A.
The DALMATIAN PRESS name and logo are trademarks of Dalmatian Press, LLC, Franklin, Tennessee 37067.
No part of this book may be reproduced or copied in any form without the written permission of Dalmatian Press,
BVS Entertainment, Inc., and BVS International N.V.

11987/Power Rangers Wild Force-Never Give Up

02 03 04 05 06 LBM 10 9 8 7 6 5 4 3 2

No one believes reports of a haunted temple in Turtle Cove, but Max, the Blue Ranger, thinks it's an Org.

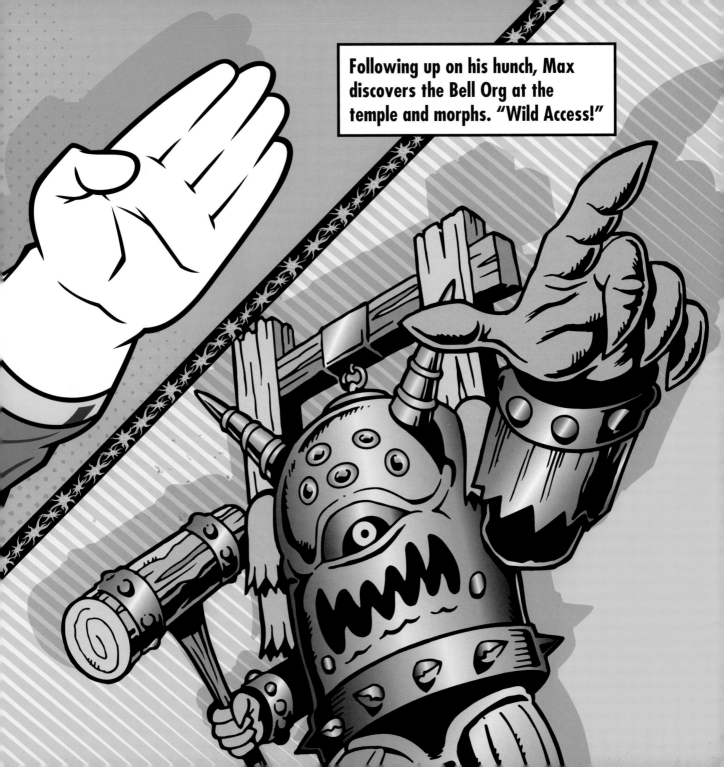

"Bell Trapper!" The Bell Org, helped by Putrids, traps Blue Ranger in a giant bell. Max drops his Growl Phone and loses his Ranger Powers!

Princess Shayla alerts the Rangers about the Bell Org and they take off to help Max.

Danny, the Black Ranger, wishes he hadn't let Max go alone. "He's my best friend. I had been afraid of heights my whole life, but when I almost fell chasing an Org, Max taught me to never give up."

The Rangers find Blue Ranger's Growl Phone where he dropped it when he fought the Org and Putrids. They know he's in trouble now!

Jindrax and Toxica appear with a gang of Putrids to try to stop the Rangers from rescuing their friend. The fight is on!

Meanwhile, the Black Ranger faces off against the Bell Org as he calls for his friend, Max, the Blue Ranger. Then he hears Max, trapped under a bell on the cliff!

"Never give up!" Danny calls out to Max, as he climbs the cliff.

Max hears Danny coming to save him, but then the Bell Org blasts the Black Ranger!

The Black Ranger keeps climbing as the Blue Ranger gains strength. "Never give up!"

Aided by the powers of Shark and Bison, Danny blasts the bell open to release Max. The Ranger team reunites: "Guardians of the Earth, united we roar!"

The Rangers combine their weapons to form the Jungle Sword and defeat the Bell Org.

Then the Rangers call the Wild Zords from Animarium. There is only one way the Rangers can fight this Org... Eagle, Tiger, Bison, Lion and Shark join together: "Wild Force—Megazord!"

Things still look bad for Animarium until the Black Ranger calls for the Megazord's Bison Kick. The Megazord kicks the Bell Trapper back at the Org, trapping him!

Trapped in his own bell, the Org is destroyed by one final Mega Roar laser blast from the Rangers' Megazord. He's toast!

Together, the Rangers will never give up. They know Toxica and Jindrax will be back...